Rodents Rule!

by Meredith Phillips

Content Adviser: Professor Peter Bower, Barnard College, Columbia University, New York, New York
Reading Adviser: Frances J. Bonacci, Reading Specialist, Cambridge, Massachusetts

COMPASS POINT BOOKS

MINNEAPOLIS, MINNESOTA

Compass Point Books
3109 West 50th Street, #115
Minneapolis, MN 55410

Visit Compass Point Books on the Internet at *www.compasspointbooks.com*
or e-mail your request to *custserv@compasspointbooks.com*

Photographs ©: Royalty-Free/Corbis, cover; PhotoDisc, 3; Norbert Schaefer/Corbis, 4; Pixtal/SuperStock, 6; PhotoDisc, 7; David Aubrey/Corbis, 8; Frank W. Lane/Frank Lane Picture Agency/Corbis, 10; PhotoDisc, 12, 14; Photospin, 15; PhotoDisc, 16, 17; Richard Stacks/Index Stock, 18; PhotoDisc, 19; Photospin, 20; Scholastic Studio 10/Index Studio, 21; Photospin, 22; PhotoDisc, 23, 24; Jean Miele/Corbis, 25; Photospin, 26, 27; Clipart.com, 28; Photospin, 28; Clipart.com, 29; PhotoDisc, 31.

Creative Director: Terri Foley
Managing Editor: Catherine Neitge
Editors: Sandra E. Will/Bill SMITH STUDIO and Jennifer VanVoorst
Photo Researchers: Christie Silver and Tanya Guerrero/Bill SMITH STUDIO
Designers: Brock Waldron, Ron Leighton, and Brian Kobberger/Bill SMITH STUDIO and Les Tranby
Educational Consultant: Diane Smolinski

Library of Congress Cataloging-in-Publication Data
Phillips, Meredith, 1971–
Rodents rule! / by Meredith Phillips.
p. cm. — (Pet's point of view)
Includes index.
ISBN 0-7565-0701-4 (hardcover)
1. Rodents as pets—Juvenile literature. I. Title. II. Series.
SF459.R63P55 2005
636.935—dc22   2004003647

Table of Contents

"From *my* point of view!"

NOTE: In this book, words that are defined in Words to Know are in **bold** the first time they appear in the text.

Who Is Your Rodent?

Origins. 4

Body Basics 6

Super Senses 8

Pet Profiles

Gerbils. 10

Hamsters. 12

Guinea Pigs. 14

Chinchillas 16

Mice. 18

You and Your Rodent

A Unique Friend 20

Needs and Wants 22

Rodent Speak 24

Equipment. 26

Animal Almanac

Fun Facts. 28

Important Dates 29

Words to Know 30

Where to Learn More 31

Index 32

Pets, Not Pests

Hello! No, no, down here. Look at the floor! Hello from the rodent world.

When you see a hamster, gerbil, guinea pig, chinchilla, or mouse, what do you think? Tiny? Twitchy? Hard to catch? We are all of that and more.

Although we find ourselves very much at home in *your* home, all rodent species originally hail from dry, desertlike places. Some rodent species still live in the wild today.

Guinea pigs were among the first rodents to be **domesticated**—they were brought from South America to Spain, where they were considered excellent pets. Similarly, chinchillas, first found in South America and prized for their soft fur, were later found to be gentle and lovable friends.

Syrian hamster

Scientists began to use us as subjects in experiments. Rodents make good subjects because we take up little space, breed quickly, and have certain systems that are similar to those in human beings. Scientists found us such a pleasure to work with that we ended up becoming their pets, too.

We rodents often get a "bad rap." People have a history of being afraid of us—probably because mice and rats are often intruders in the home. As guests, however, we can be wonderful little companions. In fact, once you get to know us, you'll understand how we can be some of the most satisfying pets in the world.

Short and Sweet

Rodents make up the largest single group of mammals, and we share one unifying feature: our teeth. We all have sharp, chisel-shaped teeth, and unlike humans, our teeth never stop growing! They grow several millimeters per week, and our lower teeth grow even faster than our upper teeth.

To keep our teeth from becoming too long, we must **gnaw** on objects to wear them down. We can actually close our lips *behind* our teeth, so that our mouths do not fill up with the material we are gnawing!

Compared to a dog or a horse, we are all small pets, but within the rodent family, we vary in size. Some of us, like hamsters or gerbils, measure 4 to 6 inches (10 to 15 centimeters) long and weigh anywhere from 2 to 7 ounces (56 to 196 grams). We can easily fit into one hand. Other rodents are two-handed pets. For example, adult chinchillas or guinea pigs are 8 to 12 inches (20 to 30 cm) long and weigh about 1 pound (0.45 kilograms).

Our wild relatives can be even larger. Beavers, a common wild rodent, can grow to 65 pounds (29 kg). The South American capybara can weigh up to 100 pounds (45 kg)!

Most rodents prefer a warm, dry climate. In colder climates, some of us hibernate, which means our bodies slow down, and we live off reserves of stored body fat. Most of us are also nocturnal creatures, meaning that we sleep during the day and are awake at night. Unfortunately, our nighttime play can sometimes disturb our owners.

What in the Word?
The word *rodent* comes from the ancient languages of Latin and Sanskrit and means "one who gnaws."

Good Sense

You will notice that when we are awake, we are active almost all the time—feeding, grooming, gnawing, and playing. Because we are small creatures, our nervous system runs at a faster pace than that of larger animals. As a result, time passes quickly for us. Our senses need to be very sharp to catch what's going on.

Hearing: You can startle us easily with a loud noise, but even a small noise can stop us in our tracks. We have the ability to hear things in high **registers** and at low volumes. Please avoid placing us next to appliances that give off high **frequencies.** These frequencies will annoy us and may even damage our hearing.

Sight: Vision is not a well-developed sense in rodents. We can't see more than a few feet ahead of us, and we are color-blind. Unlike some larger pets, like cats and dogs, we are not very good at maintaining eye contact.

Smell: Our sense of smell is vital to our lives. Smells let us know where other rodents have been, where the food is, and whether friends or foes are near. Since we use our sense of smell for so many things, it is more important to us than it is to humans.

Busy Buddies

There are many different kinds of rodents, but some of us make better pets than others. Gerbils like me are one kind to consider.

Have you ever noticed that a gerbil looks a lot like a mouse? I have the same pointy ears, whiskers, and fur as a mouse. However, my face has a slightly different shape, which is one of the ways you can tell us apart. Look at my feet, as well—they are longer than those of a mouse and are especially good for leaping and running.

I have a long, fur-covered tail that ends in a little tuft. I come in a wide range of colors: black, cream, gold, orange, or brown with a white belly. On average, I weigh 2 to 4 ounces (56 to 112 grams), and I grow to be about 3 to 5 inches (8 to 13 cm) long.

Though I am only a few inches long, I pack a lot of nervous energy into my small body. I am an active animal and can be entertaining to watch.

I am also a sociable creature, meaning that I like to interact with other gerbils and people. I definitely do not like to be left alone! It is important to keep me with another gerbil as a companion. If I live alone, I am likely to become unhappy, overweight, and live a shorter, less healthy life.

When I am not playing with other gerbils, I enjoy interacting with my human companions. I might even climb up and sit on your shoulder! Because I am incredibly friendly and easy to take care of, a gerbil like me makes an excellent first pet.

Foot Talk

Did you know I can communicate with my feet? Gerbils like me will thump a foot to warn other gerbils of danger.

Chubby Cheeks

I am a hamster. You can tell by my chubby cheeks! Like gerbils, I also make an excellent first pet. There are about 14 different kinds of hamster, and our behavior, size, and life span can vary by **breed.** Most of us who are domesticated are similar in shape and size. On average, however, I am 6 inches (15 cm) long and weigh about 5 ounces (140 grams).

For the most part, I am a **vegetarian.** I thrive on plants, grains, and fruits. I can store food for later in pouches built into my cheeks. When my pouches are full, the skin on my face stretches, and my cheeks become chubby. These pouches certainly are my most fantastic feature, and I am the only rodent who has them.

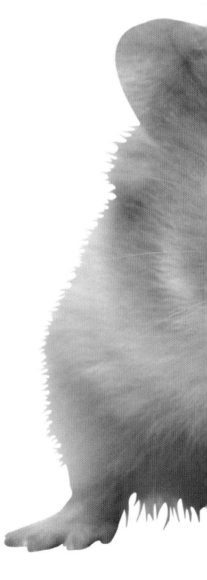

My wild relatives often blow up their cheeks to stay afloat while swimming. I, however, need to be kept dry. I need to live in a clean, dry home. If I am exposed to damp conditions, I can die.

Although I am a solitary animal and like to live alone, I do enjoy interacting with humans. I am a tender and gentle creature. I squeak, play, and am generally good-natured, but please do not squeeze me! You may harm me if you hold me too tightly. For fun, place me in a special toy called a hamster ball and let me roll around on the floor!

Before you bring a hamster home, decide which kind best suits your needs. The most common type of pet hamster is the Syrian hamster. Regardless of my variety, you'll find me easy to care for, naturally healthy, and quite amusing.

Syrian hamster

Guinea Pigs

No Ordinary Pig

My name is a little deceiving. I do not come from the African country of Guinea. I may squeak and waddle, but I am not a pig either. Truth be told, some scientists question whether I'm even a rodent—I might be more closely related to rabbits! I am a low-legged, thick-bodied animal who grows to be not quite 1 foot (30 cm) long. I weigh nearly 1 pound (0.45 kg). I do not have a tail under all the fur, so please stop looking!

I was discovered in South America. The **Incas** considered me an excellent thing to eat, but the **conquistadors** preferred to keep me as a pet. They brought me back to Spain, where I began my history as a companion animal. Over time, I have become a popular pet around the world.

If you want to become a guinea pig owner, please keep a few things in mind before you bring me home. My cage should not have a wire floor. This is dangerous to my little legs, and I may become seriously injured. Since I am approximately three times larger than a hamster or gerbil, I need a space that measures at least 18 inches (46 cm) by 30 inches (76 cm) to live comfortably.

I thrive on guinea pig **pellets,** but I also need **roughage** like lettuce or carrots. **Alfalfa** is one of my favorite treats. I need to have plenty of vitamin C in my diet, too. I can get vitamin C through a supplement added to my water supply or through certain vegetables.

I prefer to live with another guinea pig because I need lots of attention to stay happy and healthy. I welcome human attention, too, and like to play, especially in the morning and evening. Guinea pigs also rarely bite or scratch our owners, so you should feel safe around me. All in all, I am friendly and sweet and make a charming and amusing companion.

Soft as Silt

Touch me very lightly, scratching around my ears and chin. Have you ever felt anything so soft? I am a chinchilla, known for my soft, exotic fur. Please be careful, though—I have very delicate bones and don't like to be petted all over my body. I grow to be 9 to 11 inches (23 to 28 cm) long, excluding my tail, which is 7 to 8 inches (18 to 20 cm) long. Most of us weigh approximately 1 pound (0.45 kg).

I come from high altitudes in South America, but I should live inside in moderate temperatures. I like to make my home in soft pine shavings, since I am very delicate and other materials can irritate my skin or hurt my eyes. I prefer to live with another chinchilla so we can groom each other and snuggle.

When playing, I like to be free. I am very active and like to hop rather than run. I smell everything in my path. I enjoy treats as much as the next rodent—rolled oats, raw almonds, or raw sunflower seeds are my favorites—but no more than a teaspoon per day, please. Honestly, I am healthy enough sticking to chinchilla pellets most of the time.

My greatest pleasure is my bath. Get some fine, **silty** chinchilla dust from the pet store, and put it into a large bowl at least 13 inches (33 cm) deep. Then, watch me hop in, scratch, and tumble through it. The dust sticks to my fur, and when it falls off, it takes grease or dirt right along with it. Bathing like this keeps me clean and delighted.

Mice

Mice Advice

I am brown, gray, or white with beady eyes and a pointy snout. Most people find me cute. However, I can seem downright scary if I am not invited into the home as a pet—probably because for every mouse you see, there are usually hundreds more!

Mice like me are quick breeders, and we've been following people around since they began to cultivate grain, about 8,000 years ago. Wherever there is a supply of food, we can be found.

Today, so many people are interested in pet mice that there are now many different breeds, including long-haired and curly-haired mice.

You can't always believe what you see! Mice especially have a famously **adversarial** relationship with cats, but all rodents are possible prey. Please keep your rodent safe from any cats in your home.

Regardless of breed, I am very small and weigh only about 1 ounce (28 grams). While I am the smallest rodent, I am also the smelliest. Keep this is in mind when you decide which rodent is right for you!

I am wily and can slip through nearly any space, so I need to be kept in an aquarium at home. My aquarium should have a mesh top with small squares so if I do scramble to the top, I cannot escape.

Mouse pellets are the best food for me, but every now and again, you can treat me with a bit of cereal. Toys are another treat. I love them! Toys keep me active and satisfy my natural curiosity. A good toy for me is a cardboard tube from a roll of paper towels or toilet paper. No one ever said mice have expensive tastes! Little houses I can hide in or wheels I can run on are lots of fun, too.

A Unique Friend

Welcome Home

The day you get a new pet is sure to be an exciting one for you, but imagine how I feel! Whether you choose a gerbil, hamster, guinea pig, chinchilla, or mouse, try to make the transition as easy as possible. Get my cage or aquarium on the first trip. Set it up with bedding. Provide a water bottle, food bowl, nesting material, and perhaps a place to hide before you bring me home. That way you can simply slide me into my new home without any unnecessary stress.

Rodents are not used to travel, and I will need time to adjust to my new surroundings. Let me hide and be quiet for the first day. I will be in a much better mood to make friends after I have adjusted to my new environment.

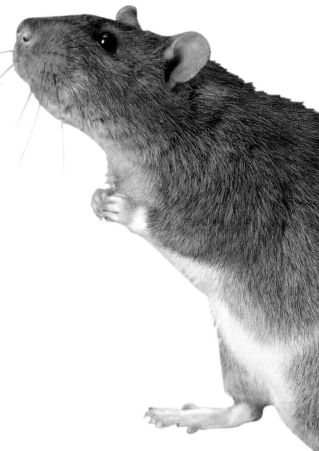

Rats can make wonderful pets, too. They are smart, sturdy, and easy to care for. Best of all, they love people!

If you already have a rodent and you are adding me to the family, do not expect too much. The other pets may not seem to be friendly at first, but that is natural for the first few days. Watch closely to be sure we are not fighting, and separate us if you see a problem.

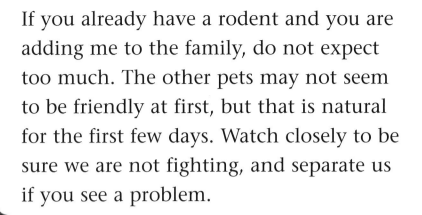

Routine Rodents

Like most people, most rodents like to stick to a routine. Try to feed me or pay attention to me at around the same time every day. If I know what to expect, I will be a healthier and happier pet.

Caretaking

For the most part, I am easy to take care of. Here are a few things you need to know about my daily care.

Make sure that I have enough clean water and food and that I am eating it, too. A good way to tell if I am sick is to check my food intake and look for problems with my waste.

Please change my bedding once a week to keep me healthy and happy. I don't like a smelly cage any more than you would! If I have a particular area I always use as the bathroom, scoop out that area every day and replace the bedding to keep things under even better control.

Picking me up helps me become tame and will eventually make me rather happy. You may have read that the best way to pick me up is by the tail, but trust me, this is not true! I find being picked up by the tail both unpleasant and disorienting. Pick me up the way you would pick up a dog or another animal— under the belly—and keep track of my feet so I feel safe.

Rodents like:
▶ Being warm.
▶ Grooming other rodents.
▶ **Burrowing.**
▶ Gnawing.
▶ Hiding.

Squeak Speak

I am easy to understand, but there are a few things that are important to watch for. Let me translate:

Noises: If I am making a lot of noise, I might be upset. In guinea pigs, though, it means I am excited to see you. Some degree of chatter is normal among rodents. After a while, you will figure out which noises are "How are you?" and which are "I'm upset!"

Movement: If I am not moving, I may be terrified. Help me move somewhere where I will feel safer, or give me some space.

Grooming: For me, grooming another rodent is like playing a board game or talking on the telephone is for you. Grooming each other is a nice sharing time.

Digestion: If I am having difficulty digesting my food, it could be a sign of a serious illness. Call the veterinarian, and take me in for an examination.

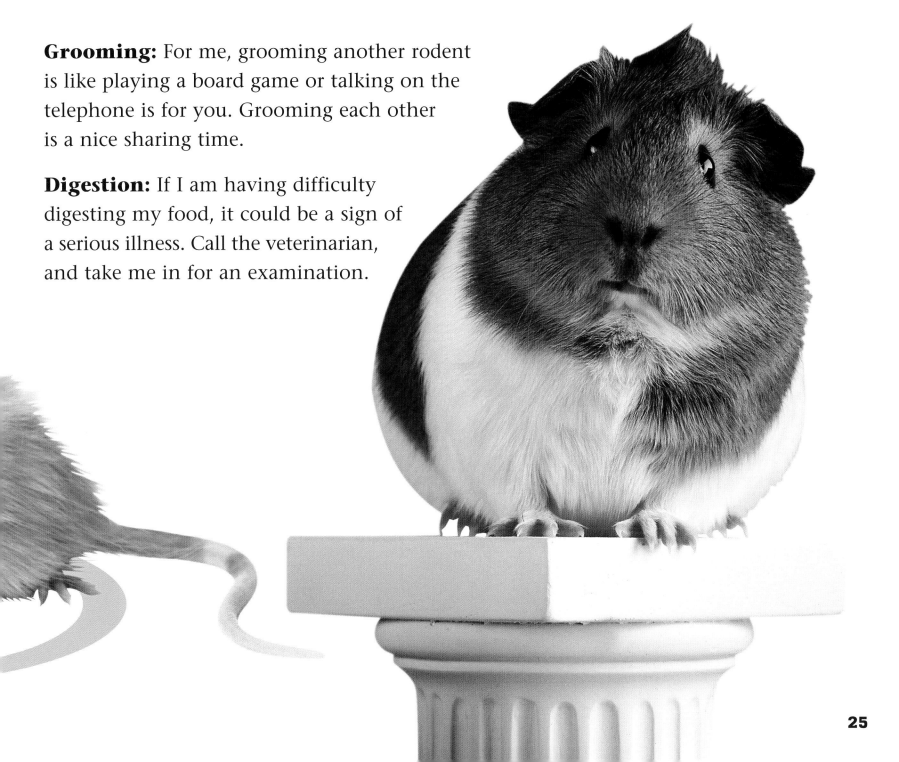

Equipment

The Stuff I Love

There are only a few things I need to remain happy and healthy.

Cage or Aquarium: First, keep in mind my size. I like to have room to stand up, run around, and hide. Second, remember that I am an escape artist, so if you decide to use a wire cage, select it very carefully. An aquarium is a safer choice, but it needs a screen top to let in air and weights on top to keep me from escaping.

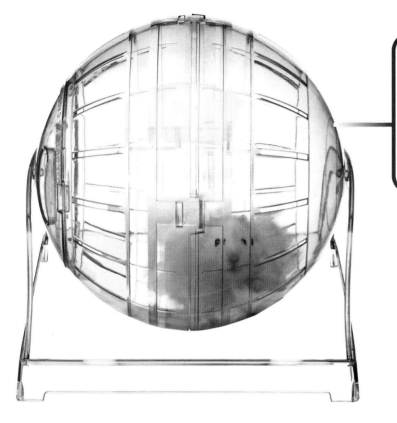

Exercise Equipment: A rodent wheel is a great tool to help me work off all my nervous energy. Please provide one I can run in comfortably. Plastic wheels are safer than metal ones.

Water Bottle: I need clean water. A bottle with a metal tip suspended upside-down is an excellent idea. Nothing can get in, and it will take me a while to gnaw through the metal.

Food Bowl: I can't help tipping over metal bowls and can't resist gnawing on plastic ones. A ceramic food bowl is probably the best choice for me.

Bedding: Bedding keeps me warm, absorbs waste, and gives me something to play with. Ask at your pet store which kind of bedding is best for me. Add to my bedding some cardboard tubes or a shoe box so I can make myself a snuggly nest.

Fun Facts Fur Real!

Where's the Beat?
During hibernation, a golden hamster's pulse drops from the fluttery 400 beats a minute to the nearly nonexistent two beats a minute, and it only breathes twice a minute!

Seconds Anyone?
Some paintings of the Last Supper have included guinea pigs as main courses.

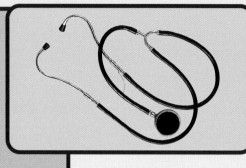

Overgrown
Capybaras are sheep-sized relatives of the guinea pig that live in South America. These gigantic animals feed mainly on aquatic grasses, though some have been known to munch through an agricultural crop or two. Picture this: They sit like dogs, they swim like hippos (with just their nostrils showing), and they party like people, with as many as 20 just hanging around at once, being social.

Home Alone
Guinea pigs are the only rodent no longer found in the wild.

Heavy Baggage
A black-bellied hamster living in the wild can store up to 200 pounds (90 kg) of food per year.

Say What?
Meriones unguiculatus is the scientific name for a kind of Mongolian gerbil. It means, in a combination of Greek and Latin, "warrior with claws."

Important Dates Timeline

8000 B.C.	1770 A.D.	1782	1930	1979	1983	2003

8000 B.C. A 1,500-pound (675 kg) rodent known as *Phoberomys patterson* lives in modern-day Venezuela and survives on sea grass.

Venezuela

South America

1770 A.D. Guinea pigs reach North America as an exotic pet.

1782 The chinchilla is first described by Moline, a Chilean naturalist.

1930 One female golden hamster and her 12 babies are taken from the city of Aleppo, Syria, to Jerusalem, where they are kept at a university. All golden hamsters stem from these original specimens.

1979 In his book, *Unmentionable Cuisine,* author Calvin W. Schwabe questions why Americans don't eat animals used as food in other countries. He cites the Arctic recipe for "Mice in Cream" and the Mexican treat, "Roasted Field Mice."

1983 The American Fancy Rat and Mouse Association is founded. Every year, the organization hosts numerous shows for rodent enthusiasts.

2003 A rodent's burrow system with nearly 2,000 fossilized nuts is discovered in Germany. The complex is more than 17 million years old, and it is believed to have been home to a species of large hamster.

29

Words to Know

adversarial: relating to conflict

alfalfa: a kind of hay

breed: a rodent classification similar to a human's nationality

burrowing: creating a tunnel or a small, snug space by digging

conquistadors: Spanish military leaders of the 16th century who claimed lands in the Americas for Spain

domesticated: accustomed to living near or with people, usually on a farm or in a home

frequencies: cycles per second of a sound wave; a sound wave's frequency determines its pitch.

gnaw: to persistently chew or bite on something

Incas: Native South Americans whose huge empire was based in Peru

pellets: small pieces of material that have been pressed tightly together for animal feed

registers: ranges of sound, as in human voices or musical instruments

roughage: food, like grain or fruits, that contains coarse substances

silty: fine-grained, like small, dusty particles of silt or soil

vegetarian: one who thrives on plant products instead of eating meat

Where to Learn More

At the Library

King-Smith, Dick. *I Love Guinea Pigs*. Cambridge, Mass.: Candlewick Press, 2001.

Kotter, Englebert, and Ehrenfried Ehrenstein. Translated by Helgard Neiwisch. *Gerbils (Barrons Complete Owner's Manual)*. Hauppauge, N.Y.: Barron's Educational Series, 1999.

Loves, June. *Mice and Rats*. Philadelphia: Chelsea Clubhouse, 2004.

Pavia, Audrey. *A New Owner's Guide to Chinchillas*. Neptune City, N.J.: TFH Publications, 2003.

Sino, Betsy Sikora. *The Gerbil: An Owner's Guide to a Happy Healthy Pet*. New York: Howell Book House, 2000.

Sino, Betsy Sikora. *The Essential Hamster*. New York: Howell Book House, 1999.

On the Web

For more information on rodents, use FactHound to track down Web sites related to this book.

1. Go to *www.facthound.com*

2. Type in a search word related to this book or this book ID: 0756507014.

3. Click on the *Fetch It* button.

Your trusty FactHound will fetch the best Web sites for you!

On the Road

The American Fancy Rat and Mouse Association
This international club promotes rats and mice as companion animals and holds many competitions and events throughout the year. For schedules and locations, please visit their Web site. *www.afrma.org*

The Belgian International Rodent Show
For the truly dedicated rodent fancier, this show travels throughout Belgium from year to year and is a giant international celebration of small friends.

INDEX

American Fancy Rat and Mouse Association, 29, 31
aquariums, 19, 20, 26

bathing, 17
beavers, 7
bedding, 16, 22, 27
breeding cycles, 18
burrows and burrowing, 23, 29

cages, 15, 19, 20, 22, 26
capybaras, 7, 28
caring for rodents, 11, 13, 15, 17, 19, 20–21, 22–23, 26–27
cats and rodents, 19
cheek pouches, 12
chinchillas, 4, 7, 16–17, 29
communication of rodents, 24–25
conquistadors, 14

diet. *See* food and diet.
digestion, 25
domestication of rodents, 4

equipment, 26–27
exercise equipment, 27
experiment subjects, 5

food and diet
    bowls, 27
    chinchillas, 17
    guinea pigs, 15
    hamsters, 12–13

indicators of illness, 22, 25
    mice, 18–19
    storage of food, 12, 28, 29

gerbils, 7, 10–11, 28
gnawing, 6, 23
golden hamsters, 28, 29
grooming, 23, 25
guinea pigs, 4, 7, 14–15, 24, 28, 29

hamsters, 7, 12–13, 28–29
handling rodents, 23
hearing, sense of, 8
hibernation, 7, 28
history of rodents, 4–5, 29

illnesses, 22, 25
injuries, 15

large rodents, 7, 28, 29

mice, 18–19, 29
movement, 24

nocturnal nature, 7
noises, 24

odors, 19, 22

picking up rodents, 23
pouches, 12–13

rats, 20
routines, 21

senses of rodents, 8–9
sight, sense of, 9
size of rodents
    beavers, 7
    capybaras, 7, 28
    chinchillas, 7, 16–17
    gerbils, 7, 10
    guinea pigs, 7, 14–15
    hamsters, 7, 12
    mice, 19
smell, sense of, 9
social rodents, 11, 15, 16
solitary rodents, 13
Syrian hamsters, 13

tails, 10, 14, 16
teeth, 6
timeline of rodent history, 29
toys, 13, 19
trivia on rodents, 28

veterinarians, 25
vision, 9

water, 20, 27
wheels for rodents, 27

ABOUT THE AUTHOR

Meredith Phillips studied literature and Japanese language at Connecticut College and is near to completing an M.F.A. in creative nonfiction at New School University. She writes about the things she loves—animals, science, books, and food. Her writing has appeared in publications, including *The Believer, The Austin Chronicle,* and *The Columbia Journal.* She also works as an editorial consultant. Meredith lives in Brooklyn, New York.